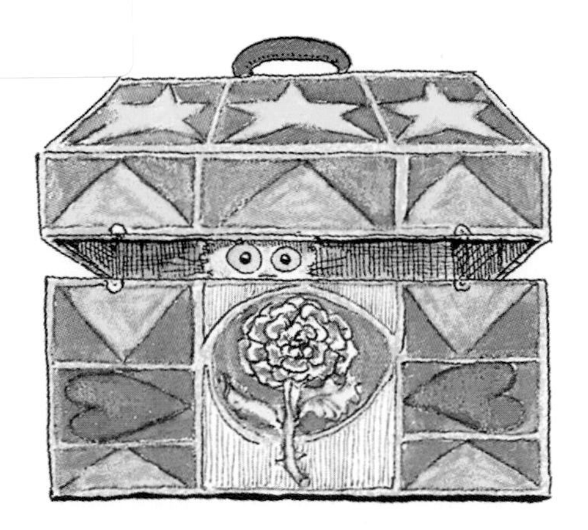

A ROSE FOR PINKERTON

STEVEN KELLOGG

PUFFIN BOOKS

PUFFIN BOOKS
Published by the Penguin Group
Penguin Putnam Books for Young Readers, 345 Hudson Street, New York, New York 10014, U.S.A.
Penguin Books Ltd, 80 Strand, London WC2R ORL, England
Penguin Books Australia Ltd, Ringwood, Victoria, Australia
Penguin Books Canada Ltd, 10 Alcorn Avenue, Toronto, Ontario, Canada M4V 3B2
Penguin Books (N.Z.) Ltd, 182-190 Wairau Road, Auckland 10, New Zealand

Penguin Books Ltd, Registered Offices: Harmondsworth, Middlesex, England

First published in the United States of America by
Dial Books for Young Readers, a division of Penguin Books USA Inc., 1981
Published by Puffin Books, a division of Penguin Putnam Books for Young Readers, 2002

10

THE LIBRARY OF CONGRESS HAS CATALOGED THE DIAL EDITION AS FOLLOWS:
Kellogg, Steven / A rose for Pinkerton.
Summary / Pinkerton's family decides he needs a friend, but is a cat named Rose really suitable?
[1. Dogs—Fiction. 2. Cats—Fiction] I. Title.
PZ7.K292Ro [E] 81-65848
ISBN 0-8037-7502-4 AACR2
ISBN 0-8037-7503-2 (lib. bdg.)

Puffin Books ISBN 978-0-14-230009-1

Manufactured in China

And another for Helen

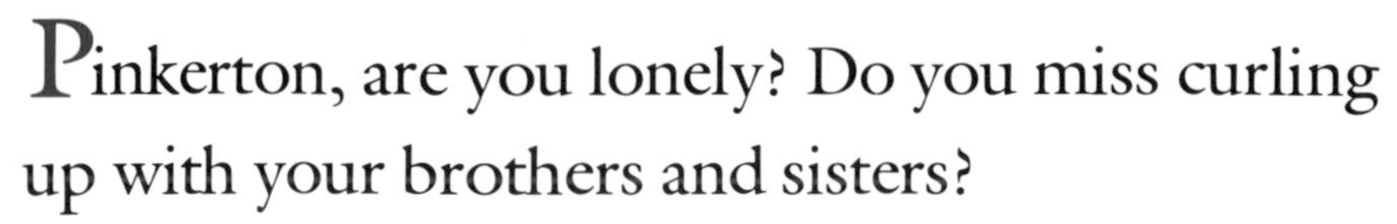

Pinkerton, are you lonely? Do you miss curling up with your brothers and sisters?

We should get some other Great Dane puppies to play with Pinkerton.

I think he's trying to tell you that he agrees with me.

One Great Dane is enough! The only other pet I would consider would be something small and quiet...like a goldfish.

This is the perfect place!

Pinkerton couldn't curl up with a goldfish.
SMALL AND QUIET PETS
clams
snails
fruit
And he couldn't play with a bird.

Maybe a kitten would be just right!

It says here in my book that Great Dane puppies and kittens can become good friends.

Here's a surprise for you and Pinkerton.
Her name is Rose.

It says in this book by Sarah Chattercat that Great Dane puppies and kittens can become good friends.

He seems to like her.
LICK LICK LICK
Purr
by SARAH CHATTERCAT
KITTENS

Rose took over Pinkerton's sun spot.
She's eating his dinner.
CHOW!
MILK
MILK
CHOW!

I think Rose wants to be a Great Dane.
Oh, no!

Now Pinkerton is trying to be a kitten!

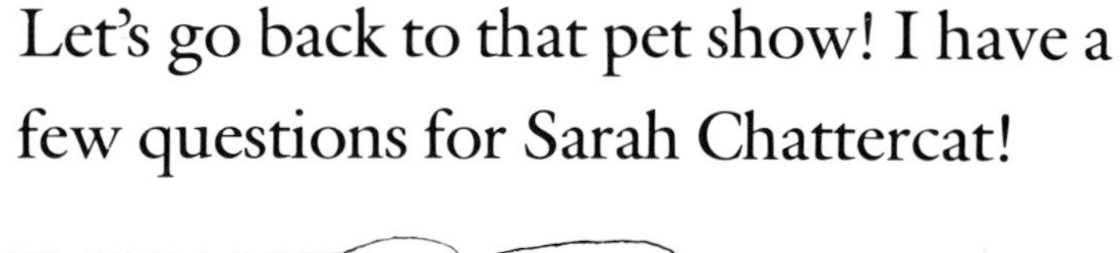

Let's go back to that pet show! I have a few questions for Sarah Chattercat!

THE INTERNATIONAL PET SHOW
ABC
TODAY'S SPECIAL EVENT
THE GRAND MARCH OF THE POODLES
DON'T MISS THE WORLD'S MOST GLAMOROUS POODLES ON PARADE

Rose! Come back!

Pinkerton will be safe with the kittens.

Help me find Rose.

Rose! Where are you?

I see her! She's in line for the Grand March of the Poodles!

I'd like to welcome our television audience to this stunning event and to introduce Dr. Aleasha Kibble of Canine University, who will present the Golden Poodle Trophy.

Stop the ceremony! Call the police! The Grand March has been infiltrated by a feline impostor!

Excuse us, but that's our cat, Rose. She used to think she was a Great Dane but she's decided to be a poodle.

Ladies and gentlemen, the crowd and the poodles have gone berserk!

They are chasing the intruding cat toward the Castle of the Kittens!

DOWN WITH CATS
POODLES
The Castle of the Kittens

There's a monster in the Castle of the Kittens.

Arrest that brute! He terrified our poodles,
and they've all fainted!

Nonsense! This wonderful dog saved the kittens.
He's a hero!

Look! It's Rose!

Does she still think she's a poodle?
Or is she a Great Dane again?
She's purring!
purr

KITTENS
KITTENS
KITTENS
TAKE HOME A SPRING BOUQUET OF KITTENS
Purr
LICK
LICK
LICK
LICK